CONTENTS

AN UNUSUAL NAME

Doctors are privileged. They get invited to children's birthday parties. Today was one such occasion. Nandita had been my patient. She was well now. A small tumour in her brain had been removed. It had turned out to be benign. She was cured and she was grateful. Today was her son's third birthday. Kids, their parents and a few friends were called over for a party. I congratulated the strapping young fellow and handed over my gift. It was a toy fire engine.

The boy's name was unusual. "Goodluck Singh Joseph", would not raise eyebrows in the north. In a Kerala home, it seemed quirky. My raised eyebrows posed the question. Joseph's elder brother took me aside. "Let me tell you the story behind the name", he said. The kids were toddling around having a great time. I settled down on the sofa with my glass of lime juice and fizz.

"It happened three years ago" he said, "during the great flood". Nandita and Joseph stayed at champathara, five miles north of Chengannur. Nandita was pregnant and due to deliver their first baby. Her antenatal checks were fine. They expected a normal delivery. It was monsoon time. The weather God had been generous. The dams upriver were full. They would have to open the sluices soon. Authorities bickered and dithered. Water was precious. Why waste it. The rains did not stop. There were floods in the plains. Water in the dams tipped over the danger mark. The dams were old and could burst. That would be a catastrophe. The authorities finally yielded. They bit the bullet and opened the sluices. The deluge into flooded rivers ripped up the banks and flooded the fields. Roads were rivers now. In no time at all, entire townships were under water. Intrepid fishermen in their dinghy's rescued people from rooftops. Sometimes they were too late.

Nandita was not scared of water. She had grown up on the banks of the Meenachil river. As a child she frolicked in strong river currents. She knew the river's pulse. The river invigorated her. She swam like a champion, caressing blue ripples with gentle swishes of her limbs. She could sense when the river was angry. This was a time to stay away from the water. Like an angry parent, the river god could lash out in fury.

She was a better swimmer than her brother who was two years older. She was also infinitely more daring. In a facilitative environment she would have bloomed into a champion. Shackles of social mores in a patriarchal society clipped her wings. She was banned from the river by the time she attained puberty. By the age of twenty she was married. Her husband Joseph was an electrical engineer. He was an excellent river swimmer too.

The torrential downpour continued unabated. Electricity was off. The phones they had had run out of charge. Joseph swore while Nandita whispered a prayer. They stood by the window of their house. What they could see, during a lull in the rain was not good. The murky waters were rising. Kerala, the land of backwaters had never seen a flood like this.

It was a natural disaster made worse by human misjudgement. Dam waters were still being released. Brimming, bulging reservoirs creaked and groaned. Surging currents downriver ripped off denuded mountainsides. The brownish virulent broth plucked feathers off civilisation. Rivers swirled toward the lakes, purulent and rich with trophies of uprooted trees and hapless fauna.

Nandita was nine months into her pregnancy. She should have been in hospital by now. She had been obstinate. She intended to stay home till her pains started. This was proving to be a bad decision. Their neighbours had scrambled for safety. Whole families ran down the fast-flooding road, bags on their heads. The bags were stuffed full of jewellery, land deeds and certificates. Nandita and Joseph had stayed on. Their house was on a hillock. They would be safe. This was another bad decision.

"We will have to leave", said Joseph. Waters were swirling higher by the minute. The road had long disappeared. Even trees lining the road were submerged. In a couple of hours darkness would descend with its deathly shroud on a now unfamiliar world. There were no lights for miles. Power stations were submerged. It was cloudy. There would be no moon or starlight tonight. To plunge into swirling waters in the dark would be suicidal. Joseph wore shorts and a T shirt. Nandita had traded her Sari for a salwar kameez. Their valuables and documents had been insulated and waterproofed. Some wedding finery and sentimental trinkets were stuffed into polythene bags and sealed. They locked all this in a steel cupboard which Joseph lashed to a window. Even if the house collapsed the cupboard would he safe. They would salvage the contents after the floods subsided. The red brick house would survive the flood. The tiled roof was liable to be washed away.

They planned their escape. A couple of miles downstream was high ground at Thiruvalla. They would float down with the current. Where the river curved, they would strike out for the shore. It would not be easy. There were eddy currents, tumbling debris and addled snakes in the water. There was no other way. God willing, they would make it. Waves were already lapping hungrily at their front door when they left. Nandita held on to Joseph's shoulder with one hand as they swam into the floods. A few tree tops peeked out of the waters downstream. Tree tops were best avoided in floods. They would be teeming with angry ants and spiders crawling up to escape the rising swell. They would repulse intruders into their oases.

The water was cold and murky as they swam across the river. A few startled looking dogs floated past. They paddled desperately to keep their noses above water. They whimpered as the water herded them to their graves. Dogs were not strong or wily enough to paddle for the shore. They were too low down in priority to be picked up by rescuers in their boats.

Joseph and Nandita swam together. Nandita held on to Joseph's shoulder with one hand. She paddled with her feet and her free hand. Joseph had suggested a rope could lash them to each other. Nandita vetoed the idea. If the tether fouled on an obstacle, they would both be pulled under. The current was strong. The way to stay alive was to stay afloat and to go with the flow.

They were close to the high ground of Thiruvalla town now. Joseph was pulling powerfully for the shore. His powerful hands churned the water in vain. Nandita held on to his shirt, matching her strokes with his. The current was far too strong. The river roared its thirst for blood. They could see a crowd near the shore watching the debris float by. There was a shout as someone in the crowd saw them. Someone screamed. Joseph waved for help.

These were spectators and not rescue workers. No one threw them a rope. No one had the courage to jump in. If Joseph and Nandita swept past, there would be nothing between them and the Vembanad lake. The rushing water cackled in sadistic derision. The river had them in his clutch. Joseph and Nandita would soon be out in the middle of the lake and beyond help. With dusk settling in, rescue was doubtful.

They were getting swept past the shoreline. Nandita saw the Sardar and waved frantically for help. She guessed he would be part of an army rescue team. The man was running down the shore unravelling his turban. It would be close. Joseph had not seen him. He seemed to have given up. He was conserving his strength for a long and desperate vigil ahead. The end of the turban cloth swished above their head and Nandita grabbed it. The Sardar had wrapped one arm round a half-submerged electricity pole, with one end of his turban held firmly in an iron fist. Nandita held on to the other and to Joseph's shirt with the other.

Snapping out of his reverie Joseph powered round to grab their lifeline. Together and in tandem, they pulled themselves in. There were some painful scrapes from a submerged concrete roof. Then they were at the cove where their saviour stood. With a powerful heave, he had them out of the water. Joseph and Nandita lay squelched on a concrete patch. The man was busy wringing out his turban when he heard Nandita groan. Nandita had gone into labour. Scooping her in his powerful arms, with Joseph running behind they headed up the embankment.

Up the hill was a mission hospital that was still functional. A makeshift ambulance was commandeered. In between her groans, which were more frequent now, Nandita turned to her saviour. "Your name Sir", she pleaded. The Sardar was bemused. He smiled and waved her on, "Good Luck" he said.

The bouncing baby boy in the brimming mission hospital yodelled. The babe announced his arrival into a turbulent world. Blissfully unaware of drama and despair his parents had been through, he proved to be a demanding irascible rascal. Nandita was soon out of the ward. She and her husband stayed in a rescue camp run by the local parish. Nandita's son was the centre of attention. "What will you name him", asked the padre. It took Nandita a moment to wipe away a tear from her eye. There was a deep sense of gratitude and conviction as she said "Goodluck Singh Joseph".

The party was getting over. Children left or were dragged home by their parents. Nandita exchanged pleasantries with me while Joseph cleared the dishes. Goodluck trudged over, lugging a fire-engine. "Well, young man. What do you want to be when you grow up?". There was no hesitation in the young man's tone. "A sardar", he said. "I want to be a sardar".

THE TAXI DRIVER

Raj Pathan was a taxi driver. His taxi, MH 1042 was of dubious vintage. His uncle, Mustafa had bought the vehicle from the Dadar bazaar. This bazaar dealt with stolen cars. Raj's car had its identity changed by the original thieves & the appearance changed by the rigors of Mumbai traffic. The engine was however vintage fiat. The car ran well & Raj was an excellent driver.

Raj was from Patna in Bihar. A minor run in with the police at Patna had culminated in his repatriation to Mumbai. Raj's family owed allegiance to Ram Bhaiya, who was an underworld don and a member of the legislative assembly. As a student, Ray dabbled in politics. He was a popular & principled student leader. When a girl student Tasleen, was molested by an IPS officer's son, he had taken up the matter with the vice chancellor despite Ram Bhaiya admonitions. The culprit had been suspended, but Ram was black listed. He was not given a seat for his post-graduation. At a loose end, he drifted into the family business. Raj & Tasleen became friends. They hoped to get married as soon as Raj could settle down.

The trouble started when Raj stole a scooter from the cinema parking lot. Stealing vehicles was fairly routine for him and he had followed the accepted business practice. He had driven to the nearest police station. Here, the cops would evaluate the vehicle & decide upon a 'tax'. With the 'tax' paid Raj would be free to modify the vehicle & then sell it in the grey market.

When Raj reached the station, the station policeman slapped him & threw him behind bars. The scooter had belonged to the policeman's brother-in-law. Ram Bhaiya had to interfere to get Raj released. The criminals and the police were both pillars of Ram Bhaiya's establishment. He could therefore tolerate little friction between the groups. Raj was exiled to Mumbai in one of Bhaiyas trucks.

Raj was a diligent worker & a gifted driver. His overt honesty was sometimes an embarrassment. One day a fat Marwari lady forget her purse with gold jewelry in Raj's car. Mustafa could never understand why Raj traced the lady to her residence & returned the goods. The lady was grateful and publicized Raj's honesty as a public interest story in a popular magazine. Neither Ram Bhaiya nor Mustafa had been amused by the turn of events.

Tasleem's parents had started pressuring her to get married to a man called Aslam. Aslam's father was a lieutenant of Ram Bhaiya. Aslam's earlier marriage and the death of his bride in suspicious circumstances did not deter the family. Aslam would be an important man in Bhaiyas machinery. The contact mattered to the family. A tearfull Tasleem telephoned Raj. An escape had to be engineered. Patna was however Aslam's home turf. With Ram Bhaiya backing him, there was little Raj or Tasleen could do.

Tasleem's brother Sharukh was sympathetic towards the couple. He agreed to help Tasleem to get away. Tasleem left the house under the guise of vegetable shopping. She hurried to the railway station, where Shahrukh waited with a small bag of clothes, some money and a ticket on a Pune bound train. Bombay trains would be under surveillance, the moment Tasleem's escape came to light. Ram Bhaiyas organization was strong at Bombay and repercussions could be

gory. Raj had been alerted by Shahrukh of Tasleem's escape. He went to Mustafa for help. Mustafa, however was curt. Ram Bhaiya had already alerted his gang in Mumbai. Raj had to run, if he wanted to live. Mustafa took the cab keys from Raj.
Raj left Mustafa's office with a heavy heart. Stepping on to the pavement he saw two tough looking goons on the opposite site of the road. Seeing Raj emerge, they moved to cross the street. A large truck blocked their way. Raj sprinted after the trunk & clung to its side as it pulled away. He was sure that the men would follow him. He jumped off the touch at the next crossing and hopped on to a bus moving in another direction. Crouching low in the bus, he made his escape.

    Raj's belongings including his mobile & money were in his room. He could not go back for them without getting shot. Raj remembered the Marwari lady, Mrs Garcha, whose jewelry he had returned. He went to the Garcha residence. The Garcha's were sympathetic, when he narrated his tale of woe. Mr Garcha had to go to Goa the next day for a meeting. Raj could act as his driver.

Wearing a cap pulled down low & dark glasses, Raj drove Mr Garcha, the next morning to Goa. At Goa, after leaving Mr Garcha he rushed to a telephone booth. Desperately, he tried to get across to Tasleem. Her mobile however was switched off. Raj thought fast. It struck him in a flash that Ram Bhaiyas men must have contacted Tasleem from his mobile. Someone pretending to be Raj must have found Tasleems whereabouts & then told her to switch off her mobile. There was no time to lose. A European couple had just parked their hired bullet motor cycle & walked towards the beach.

Tasleem was in the waiting room of Pune station. She had received a call from Raj's mobile. His voice was cracking as he spoke, but the instructions were clear. Tasleem was to wait and to keep her mobile switched off.

Raj saw that the motorcycle key was still in the ignition socket. He jumped on the bike & was off with a roar of the engine. At best, he could reach Pune in six hours. He prayed that he would not be too late.

Five hours had passed after Tasleem received her call. She switched on her cell. There was a missed call from a number she could not recognize. He tried Raj's number – his telephone had been switched off. A Barkha clad lady was coming into the waiting room. The lady looked around the waiting room till her eyes rested on Tasleem. She walked across.. Tasleem? She queried. Tasleen said yes. "Raj has gone to book your ticket back to Mumbai" said the lady.."My name is Salma & I am his friend's wife. Raj told me that you had not eaten". Despite her protest the lady laid out a mini meal of samosas and some sweet. Tasleen was hungry. She ate, eyeing the door impatiently for Raj to appear. A stranger was at the waiting room door. He signaled to Salma, who seemed to nod back. Behind him, another face appeared. Tasleen knew him too well. It was Aslam. Tasleem had been tricked. She tried to raise an alarm – But her eyes were closing with sleep. she realized that she had been drugged.

Raj parked the bike outside the station and hurried towards the waiting room. Suddenly he stopped. There were two men walking ahead of him – one of them was Aslam. Raj followed them at a distance. They stopped near the ladies waiting room. One more man joined them. Raj recognised him as one of Ram Bhaiya's enforcers. A lady emerged from the waiting room supporting a dazed and staggering Tasleem. The group headed for the car park with Aslam and the lady supporting Tasleen between them. Raj watched helplessly as they bundled Tasleen into back seat of a waiting Toyota van. There was no way he could rescue a drugged Tasleen from a bunch of armed men. He followed the quails on his motorcycle.

They were on the high way now & heading for Patna. Late in the evening the van stopped at a roadside Dhaba. Two of the men set off into the Dhaba. Raj could make out the outlines of the two ladies and the car driver. A tourist bus stopped close by. Passengers dismounted and milled about. Raj went to the van & under cover of darkness let out air from the back tire. The two men returned to the van with some packed refreshments for its occupants. The bus, with its passengers had departed. The van driver detected the puncture as soon as he moved the vehicle.

The men got out and held some discussions. Then the lady emerged with Tasleen. One of the men escorted them to a bench outside the Dhaba. The others set to work, changing the tire. Raj started up his bike and edged closer. The man, with the ladies had gone across to pick up two cups of tea. As his coasted in to the bench he saw Tasleen startle – she had recognized him.

Tasleen wrenched her arm free and ran towards him with the woman after her. The goon guarding her had not yet realized that anything was amiss. Raj picked up a large stone and threw it at Tasleen's pursuer. She fell down – blood streaming down her forehead. The goon dropped his tea glasses & groped for his gun. But Raj & Tasleen were already off on the bike, gunning down the highway. Raj knew that the gangsters would commandeer some vehicle & chase them.

He turned off the highway. They were about two kilometers away, when they came across a barricade on the road. There was a sign –Broken Bridge ahead – road closed. He looked back towards the highway & saw that a van had turned off down their road. The pursuers were on their track. Ray removed the barricade. He covered the sign with the broken branch of a tree. They drove off the road & waited behind a clump of bushes. The van came roaring down the road. One of the goons was leaning out, a gun in his hand. The van zoomed past them. Ahead was the broken bridge across a deep gorge. There was a plaintive screech of tires as the driver realized his folly. He was going too fast. The jeep plummeted into the gorge. A flash of fire erupted as the petrol tank blew up.

Raj & Tasleen rode back & turned to Goa. At the next town they brought themselves T-shirts & cut away jeans. When they reached Goa, it was past midnight. The hotel owner groggily opened the door. A young tourist couple was standing in the moon lit road. The couple registered in as Rahul & Clarissa Michael.

Rahul & Clarissa seen a restaurant of the Covalim beach. You can remember the hotels name – It MH 1042.

THE TERRORIST

Dr Mohd Abdul Rafiq was in prison. He looked around his packed cell. It was full of TADA detainees. They were a motley assortment. They were Khalid, the doctor from JIPMER, Mohammed Yusuf was a software engineer, there were five students from the Al Islam college and then of course, there was Sulaiman, Sulaiman the philosopher, their philosopher & guide and editor of the newspaper Islam today was capable of this carnage. He was an MBA from Bangalore and had been a rising star in a software firm before he gave himself to the cause. Rafiq shuddered as he remembered Sulaimans eloquence as he castigated the west for genocide of the Islamists.

Rafiq had graduated from the prestigious King Louis Medical College. He had always been deeply patriotic and was considered to be a good doctor. He had turned down more than one scholarship to proceed abroad for higher studies. Now here, he was – in jail – for an act of terror. Although he believed deeply in God, Rafiq had never worn his religion on his sleeve. It was after the carnage following religious disturbances in a neighboring state that Rafiq started attending meetings of the Islamic league. The ideals of the league had been lofty. They worked to rehabilitate the refugees. The league had mobilized funds for their resettlement. It was later that the hate messages crept in. Sulaiman had gone to Pakistan for a month's seminar. When he returned, he had become irrational. His new friends who would visit him were abhorrent. They spoke easily & casually of death & bombs. Voices of moderation were not tolerated. You were either with the group pr you were branded an infidel. In retrospect Rafiq cursed himself for conforming.

It was at one of these meetings that Sulaiman and two visitors appraised them of the planned operation. The visiting American senator was a proffered hawk. Disrupting his meeting with a protest march and smoke bombs would be a huge embarrassment for the establishment and for America.

Rafiq shuddered as he relived the moments. Sulaiman led them, with their banners proclaiming death for the infidels. They had broken through the security cordon and barged into the entourage. The terrorist who was supposed to throw the smoke bombs performed to perfection, thought Rafiq bitterly. These were not smoke bombs. They terrorists had used high-grade explosives. The blasts ripped through the spectators, mostly women & children, who had come to see the cultural programs. At least 60 were dead and many more were wounded. The police posse pounced upon Sulaiman & his accomplishes as the obvious perpetuators of the carnage. Here they were now. They were labelled and detained as terrorists and murderers. The bomb throwers had melted into the crowds.

Rafiq and the others would never breathe free again. Other jail inmates left them alone. The judges of the fast-track courts would never consider leniency or bail for the perpetuators of such heinous crimes. The interrogations started. Rafiq realized in horror that the police had been aware of everything that had transpired at their meeting. Their society had been infiltrated. He was appalled at the thought that the security agencies had been aware of their intentions. In all probability they know that the bombers would use the high explosive devices. Why on earth, did they let it happen. Sulaiman too was subdued now. Rafiq realized that he was probably as much a victim as the rest of them.

The trial made front page news in every national newspaper. The public was screaming for their blood. Fringe organizations were glorifying them as Jihadis. The court's verdict was harsh. Sulaiman, Rafiq and two others were sentenced to death. The rest of the group would serve life sentences.

The appeals by his family for clemency from the president was dismissed perfunctorily. The sentence was executed on time.

Away at a resort in Jakarta the two bombers sat sipping their cocktails. As the news of the executions flashed on the TV screens, they raised their glasses in silent tribute. It was time to plan their next operation.

THE HIJACK

Flight number IC 134 was in mid-air. The flight from Delhi to Mumbai would take Ravi 3 hours. Dinner was being served, when a scream from near the flight deck shocked the passengers. A young man had emerged from the toilet with a stocking mask over his face and a pistol in his hand. There was more commotion – this time towards the tail end of the plane. Another masked armed hijacker had his arm round an air hostesses neck & was screaming at passengers to remain seated.

Ravi had embarked the flight to Mumbai to attend a job interview at the Mazgaon docks. His engineering college professor had advised him to take at least five interview calls before setting for a job. He had finished four and had been enroute for his fifth. He cursed his luck. The woman sitting to his left was weeping silently. The fat man on his right seemed dazed – as through he could not figure out what was happening – Ravi was glad that he wasn't on an aisle seat. He had no desire for a post humous gallantry award.

Crash! The cock pit door succumbed to a hijacker's boot. They were both exceptionally well-built young men – probably around his own age – thought Ravi. He wondered how they managed to smuggle the guns & masks had been hidden in the toilets.

There must have been some collusion with some maintenance staff. He wondered what the odds to survive a hijack were.

A young man in the opposite row was whispering into a cell phone. In a trice, one of the hijackers was upon him. The butt of the hijacker's pistol caught him behind his ear. The passengers watched in horror as the young man slumped down, unconscious & bleeding.

Within minutes of the hijackers emerging, the pilot had pressed the distress button. The hijack code was alerted. The national security organizations had been set into preset activation mode. Fighter air craft had been scrambled from the nearest air field. Two Mig fighters were soon at either wing tip of the hijacked plane. They could do nothing, but provided some sense of security to the passengers.

The pilot had been ordered to alter course to Islamabad. In an hour, they would be entering Pakistani air space. The Mig's could then have to turn back. The Pakistani authorities had already been alerted. Their aircraft would take over 'nurse maid' duties after the Indian Migs turned back.

Snowcapped mountains were seen visible at the horizon. They were seen over the Himalayas. Vast stretches of snow with rocky peaks in between was all that the passengers could see from there windows. The hijackers seemed more relaxed now. The plane would soon be over Pakistan. Ravi watched the Migs veer away & turn back. The Indian authorities had apparently thrown in the towel. There would be negotiations and concessions in return for a hostage exchange. The deputy prime minister was hawkish in his political out-look. He made a call to the Air Force chief who in turn alerted a secret air force base. An Armed Sukhoi was air borne in seconds. On the national networks, the deputy premier appealed to Pakistan for safe passage in their air space.

Ravi was looking out of the window when he saw the streak of the incoming missile. The pilot saw it too. He set the air craft in a dive in a futile attempt to outsmart the missile. The missile struck, when the air craft was barely 200 feet above a snow-covered field. The plane ploughed into the field. The screams of passengers could be heard over the rending of metal. There was an explosion & then Ravi passed out.

When Ravi came to, he was lying in the snow. There was debris strewn all around. Just yards ahead was a deep precipice. Ravi guessed that most of the air craft & passengers had gone over the edge. Was he the only survivor. He moved closer to the precipice & looked down. There was a sheer drop of a thousand feet. Air craft debris & bodies could be seen at the bottom of the gorge. He heard a groan from below the cliff edge. Crawling to the edge of the precipice he looked over. One of the hijackers was on a rocky edge about 10 feet below him. He seemed to be unhurt. The ice face was sheer & without any hand holds. He could not climb up without Ravi helping him.
Ravi looked around behind him for something in the debris that would help him pull the kidnapper up. It was then that he

noticed that one of the 'rocks' in the snow was moving. He went closer. It was Neena, one of the air hostesses. She was sitting in the snow- weeping silently. Except for being acutely dazed- she seemed unhurt. Ravi helped her to her feet. He then started rummaging around the debris looking for pieces of rope and metal rods. With Neena's help he fashioned a rope out of seat-belt fragments. Using the metal rods as ice pickaxes & hanging on to the rope which Neena & Ravi passed to him – the hijacker climbed to safety. The three of them, flung together by providence sat behind a rock taking stock of the situation.

Indian authorities screamed hoarse that the hijacked passenger liner had been shot down by the Pakistan Air Force. Pakistani authorities vehemently denied the changes. It would be weeks before the air craft debris and the bodies would be recovered

There was a storm buffeting the plain. The three survivors huddled behind their rock, which would protect them from the sleet. The hijacker told them his story. His name was Mansuf & he was a final year medical student. His associate and friend –

Rehman had been a software engineer. Mansaf & Rehman had been friends since child hood. They had gone to the same schools & attended the same Karate classes. Rehman had a younger sister Noor. Noor & Mansaf were friends and planned to marry after Mansaf finished his medical education. Noor had been visiting a friend in Baroda at the time of the Gujarat riots. When order was restored in the state Noors body was found, or rather her charred remains, along with the bodies of her friend's family. Rehman & Mansur has sworn revenge. A local radical Muslim cleric had got the duo in touch with an organization. The organization had arranged for the weapons to be concealed in the aircraft's toilet by a sympathizer, whose name was ironically Ram Bhagwan. The drama had then unfolded till the interruption by the falcon missile.

The storm let up for a while, although the sky remained overcast. The three of them scrambled to collect food cans and any other items of utility they could find in the debris. Fabricating a made shift snow sledge from a twisted aircraft seat they set off – In the direction from which the aircraft had been flying. As darkness set in, they settled for the night in a cave in the rocks. Neena rationed out the food & juice bottles that they had scavenged.

It was intensely cold and they huddled together. Ravi told them about himself & his hob interviews. He spoke to them of a brother who had died at a tender age of a rare cancer. Neena too, was an only child. She had joined the airlines because she loved traveling with some experience in the domestic sector she hoped to get a job in an international airline.

An animal snort at the cave mouth jotted them out of their reverie. In the star light they could make out the outlines of a pack of mountain wolves. Their red eyes glowed like embers. Mansuf moved like lighting grabbing a rod, He charged the animals, scattering them with his sheer ferocity. Neena managed a box of matches form an emergency box & the trio lit a fire at the cave mouth. The wolves lurked at a distance but did not attack. As down broke, the animals melted away into the shadows.

The throbbing roar of chopper blades struggling in the thin mountain air brought them out of the cave. A rescue helicopter had seen the wisps of smoke & was looking for them Neena & Ravi were outside – waving whatever they could. Mansuf seemed pensive. "I suppose, I will spend the rest of life behind bars", he said. The helicopter was closing in Neena looked a Ravi who nodded ab unspoken confirmation.

The helicopter lands a hundred yards away. Two uniformed soldiers hurried to them. "Are you the only survivors" – one of the soldiers asked. "Yes" replied Neena." We are the only survivors. The hijackers and the other passengers fell in to the ravine. The trio were given blankets and food & then flown back to a base camp. At the camp the reporters crowed around.
"There were two hijackers, both were foreigners – who spoke with a European accent – Neena briefed them. As the hijacker ware stocking masks – no further details could be provided.

The trio returned to their lives Mansuf finished his medical education with honors. Mansuf & Neena were married in a quiet ceremony attended by relatives & friends, Ravi, a close friend of the family had flown in from Australia where he worked for a ship building firm. As they raised a toast to the newly-weds, Ravi smiled to himself. A chapter was over. A new life lay head of the survivers.

THE BANDIT

Raghavan Velu was a brigand and a bandit. The tribals dwelling in the high ranges of Kerala called him Anaithalavan which meant – leader of the elephants. It was village lore that Raghavan never forgot a favor or forgave an insult. Nothing & nobody could stand in the way of his vengeance.

There was a time, before his brigand days, when Raghavan was a farmer. Those were the days, when the highlands of north Kerala were dense, plush forest. Land was available, to those of strong wills and bodies or with a strong reason to be always from the shackles of civilization. A few intrepid estate owners had curved out vast stretches for their cardamom & tea plantations. Jeep tracks leading to these estates skirted the edges of the forest, which remained domain of the elephant and the tiger and their lesser denizens.

Raghavan Velu had been the heir to the Marthandom family estates. His father headed the elite emperor's guard. Raghavan trained in the martial art of Kalaripayattu & was tutored in government administration. It was assumed that he would one day occupy a position of prominence in the court of emperor of Travancore. But Raghavan fell in love with an untouchable. Her name was Shumbani and she embodied the best of genes of the Aryan & Dravidian pools. Ebony brown in her complexion she had been educated in a mission school, where her mother worked as a caretaker. She had accompanied the missionary school head mistress wife to the emperor's court, where she met Raghavan. A fiery romance issued and they were married in quiet ceremony by the missionary couple. Raghavan's family was furious. He was ostracized by the community and cast out by his family. His mastery of Kalaripayattu was well known & this saved him from being lynched.

Raghavan & Shumbani escaped in the dead of the night. They set out for the hills, where caste and creed were not issues in question. Hacking through a section of the forest, by the jeep track Raghavan made a clearing. Together they build up a house of mud & bamboo with a coconut thatch for a roof. The land was unclaimed and the forest was bountiful with resources. Raghavan hunted deer & wild bear. He could trade the skins for staples like rice in the nearby town of Kottayam. They fenced off an acre of land and started a farm. Elephants would stray into the farm & uproot the luscious plantain trees. But these were the hazards of the wild. The fragrant mountain air, exuberant in freedom was a balm for such irritants. A few other families settled near the Raghavan patch. They all had their reasons to shift to the high ranges. Most were poor and the lure of land ownership was irresistible. Soon the contingent made a visit to the Government office at Kottayam to establish their stakes. Bribes had to be paid – but the land was officially theirs. They setup a local panchayat and chose Raghavan as their representative. The land was fertile and the forest was lush. The settlers thieved & prospered. On Sunday evening a small convoy of bullock carts would set out for the Kottayam Market carrying their wares for sale. After trading on Monday, they would return with clothes, a few picture books & toys for the children & trinkets for the women. Any disputes in the settlement were arbitrated by Raghavan & his panchayat. Raghavan & Shumbani had two sons. Shumbani taught her children & a few other children in the settlement. The lack of opportunity of formal schooling for the children troubled Shumbani.

One after noon a police posse drew up at their highland settlement. A white ambassador headed the group of three vehicles. The car door opened and a prosperous looking man, gold rings glittering on his fingers, stepped out. His face looked familiar – Raghavan recognized him as a minister in the Kerala state assembly. The group seemed to recce the settlement and them left, without speaking to any of the residents. The settlers sensed trouble. They assembled outside Raghavan's hut. The minister was notorious for his land grabbing ventures. Raghavan reassured them. There was no cause for concern. The settlers had registered the land in their names and no one, not even a minister, could usurp their property. But there was a vague unease around the camp. The minister visit seemed to have vitiated the atmosphere.

A week had passed & Raghavan had almost pushed the episode to the back of his memory. He had gone hunting for wild boar & the tracks had taken him many miles away. As he crested a hill he turned back to look at his settlement. Billows of smoke were rising from the settlement. He could see crowds milling around and a few vehicles parked in the cleaning Raghavan turned & ran back to the village. It took him almost three hours to reach the settlement, or what was left of it. The house he had built with his bare hands was now rubble. Some of the other houses were burnt down. Only a few embers still shimmered in anger. There was a large group of policemen and a group of men lounging around. Raghavan looked around desperately for his family 'Raghu, Raghu' – an urgent whisper from the bushes behind him got his attention. It was Ravi, his neighbor. Ravi pulled Raghavan to a concealed place behind the bushes where the policemen would not see them. He then told Raghavan the full story.

The policemen had come in two vans. The minister had come in his white car to supervise the demolitions. Some of the residents had protested- but the police had been ruthless. Shumbani had been hit on the head by a police lathi & she had been taken to the Kottayam Medical College. Raghavan melted back into the forest shadows. He knew that the police would look for him. That was their modus operandi. All potential trouble makers would be locked up. A story would be concocted and he would be accused of setting the settlement of ablaze. They would remain in protective custody till the issue was forgotten by the public & by the press. There was a jeep track on the other side of the hill. Raghavan ran to the track. An estate jeep should be coming down the road soon.

A jeep laden with estate workers was coming down the road. Raghavan put out his hand & the jeep stopped – the driver could always accommodate another fare. The land grab by the minister was the focus of conversation. They had heard that a timber baron had paid the minister for the land. Raghavan pretended to know nothing of the incident. His priority was to see Shumbani.

He found Shumbani in the post operative ward of the Medical College. There were tubes everywhere. She was barely conscious but seemed to recognize her husband. For three days and nights, Raghavan sat by her bed side. The boys were now with Shumbani mother. It was almost a month before Shumbani could be discharged home. She was stronger now & could walk with help. The boys had been enrolled in school by their grandmother. Raghavan realized that Shumbani would not be able to cope with forest life again. He thrust aside his thirst for vengeance, working in the field & chopping wood for a living. As a laborer he would be inconspicuous. He now had both the police and his own estranged kin after his blood. He rarely read the newspaper and lived from day to day finding happiness in the wife recovery & his son's education.

One day Raghavan had gone to Kottayam town to get his axe sharpened at the local lathe. He chanced upon a political meeting. He was shocked to find that it was the same minister – who had got the settlement gutted – who was addressing the crowd. Raghavan climbed the wall of the maidan & edged closer to listen. The minister speech was almost over, and a few reporters were asking questions "I have dedicated my life to the cause of the poor" – the minister was in reply to a question. "I will not rest till every Keralite has a roof over his head & a yard to keep his cow". The applause from the crowd was deafening. Raghavan edged closer to listen. A reporter owing allegiance to an opposing political alliance was asking a difficult question. Some of the ministers' goons heckled him & tried to manhandle him. The minister quietened the crowd. The reporter wanted the minister's version of the incident in the high ranges where fifty settler's homes, were burned and the residents beaten. The minister smiled as Raghavan seethed in fury, his hand gripping his sharpened axe. "There was no settlement." The minister told the crowd. There was a brothel run by a man called Raghu which, I shut down. You must be upset because you were a favorite customer". The reporter was being heckled.

Something snapped inside Raghavan. With a roar, he somersaulted over the policemen guarding the podium. The sharpened axe swished in the air. There was a thud as the ministers severed head hit the platform. His lifeless body – still clutching the microphone, followed. Raghavan flicked up the severed head with his foot & held it up for the crowd to see. He then spat on it & kicked it into the air like a football. No one made a move, the axe dripped blood and the wielder was obviously a master of war. Raghavan sprinted for the 15-foot wall behind the podium & vaulted over it, before the first policemen moved. Policemen who ran around to the spot found no trace of him. The killer identity remained a mystery which was never solved. A foreign hand was suspected by the police and five college students rounded up as co-conspirators. This was the secret of governance; The establishment gained political mileage from every adversity.

Raghavan made his way back to the hills. We wished to see his family once more- but did not want to leave a trail which might incriminate his loved ones.
There had been many changes, since he had left his forest abode. The lush forest, where the settlers had camped had been denuded of trees. A huge logging operation was in progress. Behemoth trailers lugging huge logs of teak wood polluted the forest air with sulphureous fumes. There was huge lumbar yard, where Raghavan's settlement had stood. There was a fueling pump for the trucks. There were some shops selling

cigarettes and soaps toddy shop stood where he had built his house years ago. Raghavan walked into the toddy shop. Pretending to be a wood cutter looking for a job, he quizzed one of the security men, winding down over a couple of bottles of toddy.

The equations and economics were explained to Raghavan. 50% of the total proceeds went to the minister and his friends leaving 20% for the police and 30 for the contractor. As the wood belonged to no one, explained the security man – everyone was happy.

Raghavan Velu was on the path of retribution. That night, the loggers camp went up trucks sent up an orange plume which could be seen as far as Kottayam. The guards claimed to have seen a giant of a man with a flaming touch in one hand and a blood-stained axe in another, flitting from building to building setting them ablaze. They had fired their guns but to no avail. The legend of the Forest Brigand was born.

The government instituted an enquiry into the incident. The committee made starting conclusions. The brigand & his men they alleged, had denuded vast stretches of forest. Some police trucks tracking the brigand were burned by the gang. A brigade of the army was provided to protect the lumber contractors. Platoons of special forces units were sent on Raghavan's trail. But Raghavan was too smart for them. The forest was his home & the road to the hills hemmed in by culverts and rocky overhangs. No lumbar truck made it safely through Raghavan engineered rock slides and road blocks – the illicit lumbering ground to a halt. Raghavan remained an enigma. His family did not know that he was the forest brigand although they suspected that he had a role in the minister death. The boys were growing older now. They had both been selected on scholarships to an elite hotel management course.

The state ministry was troubled. The illicit revenue from the lumbar trade was getting stifled. Party members had their children tutoring abroad and hooligans had to be paid. The democratic process would suffer if the brigand continued his stifling grip on the hills. Helicopter patrols and special service personnel was on his trail now. The government version was that there was a band of terrorists, about 200 strong and heavily armed who were using the hills as a training camp. The band was blamed for a school bomb in Kashmir, a railway coach fire Godara and an out-break of food poisoning in Mangalore.

Raghavan escaped the police cordon to a village in Tamil Nadu. Greasing the palms of a few officials he had documents to prove that he, Tengu Velayudan had resided in the Araccad village since his birth, as had father before him. He started a small tea shop, which thrived. His hard work paid off. The tea shop expanded to a three-star hotel within a few years. He got back in touch with his wife Shumbhani. The hotel thrived. His sons and wife accepted him without too many questions. Soon his children joined him. They started a chain of hotels. The hospitality group they founded soon stretched across and dominated all of South India.

Raghavan velu alias Velayudan was retired now. He lived with his wife Shumbani in a modest house in Tamil Nadu, while his sons ran the hotel chain. The mornings paper grabbed his attention. "The Forest Brigand is Dead". – the headlines screamed.

A posse of policemen lead by the Inspector Pundha – a nephew of the railway minister had cornered & killed the forest brigand in a fierce encounter. Raghavan smiled to himself. Democracy & the rule of law had won a well-deserved victory. An era was at an end.

THE FIRE MAN

Ram Singh joined the fire department as an apprentice when he was 18 years old. He had initially tried for enrollment in the state police. The asking rate for the police department was too high. His family could not cough up the Rs 75,000/- for the coffers of the party in power. Jobs in the fire department cost less. His maternal uncle, who had sponsored Ram's education had paid 20,000/- for a certificate stating that Ram had passed his 12 th class and another Rs 30,000/-, to get him selected to the department. But a government job was an insurance for the whole family. The dowry he would earn at his wedding would be substantial. His uncle's investment was considered money well spent.

The two years of Ram's initial training was at the fire fighter's academy. The course was surprisingly well conducted & professional. There were theory lectures in the basic sciences which was to be followed by training in fire-fighting methodology. The directors were obviously aware of the quality of education in the state and how easy it was to get pass certificates. Ram found the classes interesting. He was physically fit & with his newly found zeal for studies he did well & graduated with honors.

His uncle was soon demanding that his loan be returned. He had a daughter of marriageable age. His son was mediocre in academics and would need a management seat in the engineering college. Ram set aside a part of his salary to pay back his uncle.

Ram found a sea change in the cultural professional ethos when he moved out of his training institute and to the fire department unit. The idealism & zeal were missing. He found himself with a group of potbellied alcoholics who seemed to have a zest for everything except their jobs. The men worked in 8-hour shifts under the supervision of controller. Ram soon realized that a good percentage of the fire fighting force existed only on paper. These fictitious fire men's salaries were diverted to the parallel economy of Patna.

The charter of duties of the fire station included six monthly certification of all the commercial enterprise promises as fire safe. The levy collected for the issue of these certificates was again diverted to the various rungs of the collection chain. Most of the establishments found it cheaper to pay the six-monthly toll. A multinational company had tried to buck the system. They had installed a state-of-the-art firefighting system & had refused to pay any under the table bride. Their shop had been gutted one night. Although connivence of the fire department was suspected nothing could be proven. Patna city lived by its own rules. The company moved its office to Kabul, where the rule of law was more rationally enforced.

There were a few real fires where the fire trucks had to roll in. Ravi loved those challenges. He was invariably in the fore front, risking his life – much to the amusement of his colleagues. Ravi also turned down his share of the department's illicit taxation. This act of defiance caused some consternation up the hierarchy. How ever they soon realized that he was harmless. He seemed motivated by an edifice of misplaced values which his colleagues were sure would crumble. He had camaraderie with and concern for his colleagues. It was unlikely that he would cause any major ripples or instigate an enquiry. There were honest fools- even in Patna. They were tolerated as long as they did not rock the boat.

Ram was a good firefighter & his work was appreciated. On two occasions he had rescued people from burning buildings, seconds before the structures collapsed in piles of ashen rubble. Once he jumped from the third floor of a burning building holding a rescued infant in his arms. Press photographers had covered the event & the political powers had to oblige public expectations by awarding Ram a medal. This caused considerable consternation as the minister had already promised to medal to Dhaku Somnath's nephew whose name figured in the rolls of the fire department and who diligently collected his pay & cuts monthly from the departments office.

Ram managed to save enough money to arrange his sister's marriage. The dowry demands of his in laws however continued to bleed him. He had to sell his ancestral house and move with his mother to the firemen's government quarters. Ram himself was in no hurry to plunge into matrimony. He had sworn, not to accept dowry. Besides, his line of work was risky and he worried that the bondage of wedlock would hold him back from the risks, which his duty demanded.

Ram was too much of a celebrity to be denied his promotions. In due time he was the chief fire officer of the precinct. As the chief fire officer of the station, he had to co-ordinate the collection of grey taxes. That was how the trouble started. When the establishment owners sent their representatives with their half yearly donations – Ram send them back. He decided to inspect the buildings himself. Ram was appalled by what he saw. The local cinema theatre did not have a single operational fire extinguisher. The fire escape had long been modified to accommodate a cigarette shop. The electrical wiring had been redone on many occasions and most fuse boxes were redundant. Ram was appalled at the state of affairs. The delivered an ultimatum to the business owners. Some safety standards would need to be met. If not, he would close their places down. Some of the business men suspected that all this was a ruse to hike the illicit fire tariff. They send emissaries with extra money. Rams turned them away curtly

Ram's sisters marriage was crumbling. The boys demand for money were unsustainable. Ram's house had already been sold and there was little he could do to assuage the boy's greed. One day his sister ran away from her in laws house. She stayed with Ram & their mother. But Ram was firmly of the view that a woman's place was in her husband's home. Although he loved his sister dearly, he forced her to return. He accompanied his sister back to her husband's house, apologizing on her behalf, entreating them to accept her back. Ram had withdrawn some money from his provident fund, which he gifted to his brother-in-law. Tempers were assuaged, at least temporarily.

The cinema theatre was owned by a political goon, through a 'front' man. Ram's inflexible attitude was making him unpopular with the political patrons. When the central fire board over ruled Ram's objections on the abject neglect of fire precautions, Ram lead a team of journalists, who photographed and published details of the flagrant violations. The minister called a secret meeting of his crisis management group. A plan to ensure Ram was engineered.

Fortunately for Ram, one of his reporter friends got wind of the conspiracy. The agent who came in with a bag full of currency was apprehended before he could reach Ram's office. His mobile telephone was confiscated and contacts traced to the minister's office. The resulting scandal claimed a few political scalps. But public memory is short. The press could not protect him forever. Within 6 months Ram was posted to a newly created appointment. His office would be five hundred kilometers from Patna. Ram could not leave Patna. His mother refused to leave the town & his sister's marital woes refused to resolve. Ram was left with no option, but to resign.

Ram's resignation from the fire department emboldened his sister's in laws. He would soon have to vacate his government house. With whatever money he gets from the department, he bought a small house for himself & his mother. His brother-in-law was furious. He wanted the money for his business.

One morning Ram received a desperate call from his sister imploring him to come quickly and save her. The telephone connection had been cut abruptly. Ram got on his jeep and covered the 60 km distance to his sister's house in under an hour. From a distance, he could see smoke billowing out his sister's bedroom. Her husband and a group of neighbors had collected in the garden, but seemed to make no effort to extinguish the fire or rescue any one inside the room. Charging in, Ram kicked open inside the room. Charging in, Ram kicked open the door of his sister's bedroom. He saw with horror that it had been locked from the outside. His sister was lying unconscious near the window, which she had been trying to open. The window had been nailed shut by someone. Ram charged in through the fire and smoke & scooped his sister up in his arms. Running out with her, he hailed a passing vehicle to rush her to the nearest hospital.

The surgeon was sympathetic and competent. Most of her body had suffered burns. The chances of a 90% burn surviving was miniscule. Despite all possible medical attention, after hovering on the brink, her body racked with pain for three days, she passed away. Ram remained at her bedside trying to help her through the ordeal. Her in laws did not visit her in hospital. They had bribed policemen investigating the case. A doctor had been bribed to certify that she was in delirium and unfit to give a statement. Ram knew that this was not true. His sister had been perfectly coherent till a few hours before her death. The investigating police team, filed a report of suicide. Ram knew the real story. Her harrowing tale of being beaten, set on fire and then being locked up in her bedroom would haunt him forever. Ram conducted his sister's final rites alone. His sister's in-laws, who were already out of lockup refused to attend the function.

That night, Ram paid a nocturnal visit to the in-laws bungalow. The front door was locked, but there seemed to be a conference of sorts in progress. Five cars were parked outside the house. Methodically Ram emptied the petrol from the vehicle's tanks & splashed it all around the house. The air conditioners of the house would prevent the petrol fumes from alerting the inhabitants. There was an electric pole near the houses entrance. Shimming up the hole he cut a wire and connected it to the house's decorative perimeter fence.

The front door opened. The petrol fumes had possibly alerted someone. Nonchalantly Ram flicked in a lighted match into the court yard. There was an explosion of flames as the petrol fumes caught fire. There were screams as people tried to escape. His brother-in-law charged for the fence. His clothes were on fire. He made it to the fence – but was thrown back by the electric charge flowing through it. Ram stepped back into the shadows to watch the dance of death.

Clang – Clang – a fire engine was drawing near. The fire fighters were seen rigging up their hoses. Ram stepped out of the shadows. One of the fire men recognised him. This was the way it had always been. Ram would always turn up for fighting a fire even if he were off duty. Don't touch the gates – he advised them. One of the over head wires seems to have snapped. He helped the team disconnect the fishes and then to douse out the embers. The firemen were grateful and thanked him for helping out. Everyone in the house was dead, but the conflagration had been contained.

A reporter was asking Ram- `Sir – why were you firefighting. We know that you had resigned.

Rams answer was clothed in sadness – He said – "Once you are a fire man – you always remain one.

THE ATHEIST

The youth was a rebel in every sense of the word. He rebelled against authority, as a kid he rebelled when he was asked to drink milk, as he grew up he rebelled against home work – against the school uniform & against his mother when she refused him permission to stay back after school for football. Maybe it was the diet of fresh fish curry & rice, against a back drop of communism & student unrest or the relative isolation of growing up bereft of the sobering influence of friends or siblings.

There was a veritable library at home, for father had been an arm chair philosopher whose tastes in literature ranged from Dante to Gordan & PG wood house. The effect of uncensored literature or a developing mind contributed to his non conformism.

A natural extension of rebellion against human authority is the questioning of the heavenly one – and by the time the youth was in college, he was a professed atheist. Religion – the opium of the masses was invented by smart men to control the proletariat, he averred. God was a figment of one's imagination, a creature of convenience and the vicarious enforcer of a code of conduct which suited big brother.

The youth would sprout Darwinian hypothesis on the evolution of the species. He had his own pet theory on the origin of the universe. If a negative and a positive could nullify each other result in a Zero – surely a universe and an anti-universe could be evolved from nothingness. No argument could sway the youths convictions and the elders would turn away muttering – "arrogant fool".

As time is the best healer – it is also a great modulator of excesses. With passing years, the youth was tempered by influences both good and bad to the realization and acceptance of powers and concerns beyond his own. His active atheism merged into an agnosticism which later evolved into acceptance and dependence in the power, presence and compassion of the almighty.

He tended to pray more and soon realized that Divine intervention often occurred before he appreciated the gravity or significance of issues. Threats were thwarted before he was aware of their existence. The most dire of dangers were the ones he was unaware of. The youth's conviction of the lack of God and in his own infallibility were both eroded by the passage of time. Failures and frustration mellowed the euphoria of youth into the wisdom of years. Occasionally he would muse over his earlier pet theories on the evolution of the universe. There was a certain pride in the reminiscence on the originality of thought at a tender age.

It was during one of those moments of unconscious self-appreciation that he remembered the first few lines of the book of Genesis – "In the beginning there was nothing – and out of nothing is God created the heavens and the Earth" – The youth realized that he had not been so original after all.

THOPPIL ISLAND

Rain and the River:

The Lord of the river opened an eye. There was a splash as the boys jumped in. They swam naked leaving their shorts on the river bank. Schools were closed. The monsoon was setting in. A storm was brewing. Heavy rains had been predicted by the meteorological society. For once, they seemed vindicated. Floods would come, turning the paddy fields into one giant lake. Major embankments around the fields were still above water. They would soon go under. Then, it would be impossible to walk to the river. Fish farms by the river's edge would be flooded. Farmed Fish would swim away. Kuttan was out with his net. He would catch as many of them as he could. There would be another bonanza for him when the floods receded. Water would gush back out of the flooded fields and into the river. Strategically placed nets and baskets would trap fish.

The boy and his friend Ravi lived on the hill overlooking the fields. They ran down barefoot from their homes, racing to reach the river first. They learned to swim here, with hollow coconuts as floats. The boatman had been an inspired if impatient coach. They learned to fish. The boys were soon out of the water and ready for fishing. Bamboo sticks made the best fishing rods. Nylon thread and fish hooks were bought from or gifted by Ravi's father's shop. For bait they had earthworm. There were worms in the ground where wash water from the kitchen drained. The boys poured salt water in the mud. Worms wriggled out and were stuffed into a jam bottle. At the river's edge they would thread worms on their hooks. Floats were made with tender tapioca shoots threaded on and tied to the nylon threads.

They sat by the riverside intently watching their floats. A dip in a float showed that fish were biting. When the hook stuck, the fish would dive, taking the float down. If the boys were not alert and the fish large enough, their fishing rods would disappear down the river. There was a howl of delight from Ravi. His float plunged as a large fish took the bait. The rod was almost wrenched out of his hand. A deft flick of the rod reaffirmed his skills and redeemed Ravi's honour. The thrashing silver fish landed on the grass. The boy pinned the fish down with his towel while Ravi extracted the hook. They covered the fish with an inverted basket.

There was a gash on Ravi's finger. The hook had lanced it when he pulled it off the fish's lip. Drops of crimson blood spattered the grass. "What have you done?" Lakshmi the laundry woman was walking past. She washed Ravi's hand in river water. Tearing a thin strip of cloth off her lungi she applied a firm bandage. The bleeding stopped. While all this was going on, the boy lifted one edge of the basket and peeped in. It was a large fish. It's thrashing had stopped The fish opened a weary eye and looked at him. He was alive, but just about.

All attention was on Ravi's finger. With a flick of his foot, the boy returned the fish to the river. For a moment, as the fish floated up on his side, he thought it was too late. Then, there was a small wiggle of movement. The fish came to life. He dived, came up, wiggled again and then swam away. The boy moved downstream and splashed into the river again. Ravi would think the fish escaped on its own. There was a plop by his side. The fish had come to say thank you. They looked at each other for a moment. Blinking his large eyes, the fish dived away.

Ravi was standing by the basket. "Where did you go?" he asked accusingly. The blighter got away. The boy was apologetic. He would show Ravi his stamp collection. He would let Ravi ride his new red bike. Ravi was pacified. It was time to head back. As the boy turned away to tug on his mud-spattered khaki shorts, there was a warm glow in his chest.

It was raining now. The river rumbled. Soon, the water would be unsafe for swimming. Currents would get tricky. There would be little whirlpools. The smaller whirls were innocuous. Larger ones could suck you down. Kannan who lived in the rubber estate had the deformed foot. The deformity was by birth. Local lore was that his foot had been twisted by a whirlpool in childhood.

There were crocodiles in the river. They would grab a chicken or a calf that ventured too close to the river's edge. A cow who had rushed to her calf's rescue had been drowned and devoured by a large crocodile living under the Kollad bridge. Attacks on humans were rare now. Industrial waste had poisoned large swathes of the river. Fish drifted away. The crocodiles followed.

Flood in the monsoon season was a yearly feature. The past three years had been drier. Monsoons were feeble. Roads were rarely underwater. Floods barely managed to wash out the tangled masses of water hyacinth into the backwaters. This year was expected to be different. The met department predicted an ultra- generous deluge. It seemed today, that they might be right.

The boys were out of the river and running back. They raced each other down the embankment. The rain lashed them in all it's fury. At home his mother chased him down, chastised him and dried him with a thin cotton towel. She then rubbed powdered pepper into his scalp to keep off the cold. These home remedies were effective. The boy once lacerated his bare foot on a sharp stone in a muddy field. Pappu, the toddy tapper, who was there, made him pee on the wound. A warm aseptic deluge cleared away the mud and dung. The wound healed well. Sepsis and Tetanus were rare. The boy was fully immunised. His mother had been diligent. Tetanus had been a major scrounge a generation ago.

Lunch was delicious. Rice and dal and fish curry. There was a lull in the downpour. It still drizzled. A few miles west, over the sea, storm clouds were building up. The boys ran round the coconut grove. Ricki, their dog, ran with them howling in excitement. There were mango trees to climb. Ricki chased a rat down it's hole. Rat holes could be dangerous. Sometimes the tenant was a snake who had gobbled up the incumbent.

Rikki's sense of smell could fail him. Snakes, unlike rats had no distinctive smell. They sensed movement with their eyes and vibrations with their forked tongues. Snakes stored memories in their DNA. Wise farmers never killed snakes. Snakes kept the rat population in check. If you killed a snake and dumped his body, you were in trouble. The snake's mate would come and read the memory engraved in the dead snake's eyes. And then, he or she would get after you for revenge. If you had to kill a snake you burnt the carcass. This denatured the DNA code and destroyed the photographic evidence recorded in the eyes.

Theboys played football across the mud puddles. The rubber ball was heavy and had a mean bounce. You could get concussions if you headed the ball too often or too hard. It was teatime. Mom would be yelling for them soon. The boy's clothes were filthy and caked. There was mud all over them. Rikki's paws were caked in wet goo. There was a well in the yard. Ravi and the boy took turns drawing water and doused themselves down. If he muddied up the rooms, he would be a tongue lashed and cane whipped.

The boy sat out on the porch with his father. Dusk was settling in. Battalions of bats cruised overhead. Bats were nocturnal creatures. They navigated and hunted using their sonars. Their nightly peregrinations decimated rat regiments in the nearby forest. The bats would be back in the morning. Through the day they slept. You could see them, hanging upside down from the giant, gnarled Banyon tree in the temple yard. They were fat, furry and ferocious looking creatures.

No one disturbed them. They were part of the temple ethos. They added to the mystique of the temple. They were believed to be under the deity's protection.

Stars tumbled out from a rent in the clouds. An odd satellite drifted by recording the storm. A shooting star whizzed across to a lonely death in the clouds. Dinner was ready. In the yard fireflies feted a lull in the storm and lit up a mango tree. By morning they would be dead, churned in the incandescence of fame. Frogs croaked in a nearby pond. Crickets chirped. A dog howled in the dark. The next house was a furlong away. You could barely spy their petromax lamp on a clear night.

There were spirits in the dark, good ones, naughty ones and nasty ones. Good spirits were generally benevolent and a bit lazy. They would plant a trough of mushrooms in your yard or make the jasmine bloom. They blessed the mango trees in season and pineapples round the year. You could sense their presence. They protected the boy's feet from snakes, scorpions and tiger ants when he ran barefoot through the brush.

The evil ones generally left you alone, unless you messed with them. The neighbourhood was abuzz with rumours that Parushi the witch did black magic. She used spirits to settle scores and to start fires. If someone's cow died or a goat fell into a well there would be whispers about Parushi. Most people left evil spirits alone. If you encountered a demon, you just ignored him or her and went about your business.

Kuttichathans were naughty critters. They had great energy. Chathans would startle you in the dark, rain pebbles on your roof or scare your cow so that her milk would run sour. They would mix up good and bad coconuts you sorted the day before. Some magicians enslaved kuttichathans. You put a magic rusty nail in a kuttichathan's head and he was under your orders. Chathans resented control and looked for an opportunity to escape.

An enslaved kuttichathan once coaxed a magician's wife to pull the nail out of his head. The poor lady knew neither her husband's vocation nor the identity of her servant. She pulled out the nail. The Chathan escaped after turning all the chicken in the farm barren. There were other mythical tales about chathans. There is enough material on chathans to fill a large book or to make a movie. It was rumoured that a grand magician, tired of the chathan's indefatigable energy, send a horde of them to the seashore to count waves. It keeps them busy to this day.

The boy had his own brush with the spirits. In the dark trees behind his house he once saw a giant snake with the head of a man. He never told his dad. His father was fearless. He would go and investigate. The boy was very fond of his father. The snake would not harm a boy. He could hurt his dad. Spirts and apparitions had a code of honour and of conduct.

The boy was not afraid of the spirits. Horror movies and ghost stories did not frighten him. A city cousin had lent him a few vampire and Dracula comics. The tales bored him. Legend was different from fiction. Sanitised horror stories for city snickers lacked authenticity. Boys from towns could not feel the pulse and throb of forces that shaped the world. Legend was what bound you to the land. The boy sensed he was part of it. He waited for the show to start, for legends to unfold.

A nippy breeze, fresh from its tangy foray over the seas whipped around the house. Thunder rumbled in the distance. You could feel the wall of rain weighing down across the paddy fields. In daylight hours you often saw the rain start. There would be a pillar or two of rain. These pillars stretched from the ocean and to the clouds. Sometimes the pillars were so thick and dense that fish could swim up them. They stayed up in the clouds. These fish would drop when the clouds burst. In lakes, high up in the hills you would occasionally find them. Survivors from cloud nine.

Pillars of water would soon be bridged by walls of the torrential downpour. The lumbering downpour would then bear down with fire and fury. The boy had watched this spectacle often. Tonight, the storm was intense. It was a tropical storm in all it's splendour. Tree broughs creaked and cracked. Leaves and fruit were hurled about in splattering fury. The sky erupted in fireworks as lightning and thunder rent the cloudy shroud. The rain started. A cascade or an avalanche of water poured down from heaven. The lights were off. Mother lit a candle.

Dinner was a hurried affair. They had not stocked up on candles. Mom was not too keen to do dishes in the dark. He helped mother to clean up. She did not trust him with the dishes. The boy retired to his room. There was mini mayhem there. One window latch had popped open. His bed sheet was drenched. The blanket and mattresses were dry enough. He spread the blanket for a sheet and covered himself with a table cloth. He glowed with excitement. He knew instinctively that tonight was the night. He had a pact with Ravi. It was best to grab some sleep while he could. The hands on the luminous dial glowed and glowered. It was past nine. Midnight was just three hours away. He closed his eyes.

Adventure at midnight:

It rained and it poured. The constant patter of rain drops was punctuated by peals of thunder. He slept through it all. It was past midnight when he sat up in bed. For a moment he was confused. Then he heard the knock again. Pat,Pat, someone was knocking at his window pane. He opened the window. Ravi stood there. Ravi had wrapped a fluttering sheet of plastic around himself in a futile attempt to keep dry. "Come", he whispered. "Let us go down to the field". The waters have risen and we have a boat.

The boy grabbed a cap and tugged on an old brown jacket. He gingerly opened the front door and stepped out.

He paused and listened for a while. Mom and dad were still asleep. He and Ravi scampered down the hill to the paddy fields. Somewhere, a dog barked. The boys did not care. It would take more than a couple of local boys to bring the dogs out of their shelters in this kind of weather. They were at the bottom of the hill now. Ravi was right. The river overflowed its banks. There was a large lake where the paddy fields had been.

A paddle boat was tied to a coconut tree. The boat bobbed about in the water and seemed to beckon them. The boat belonged to Ravi's uncle. Gopi was a boatman at the government ferry. He kept this boat near his house for fishing and for catching crabs at night. Gopi had a weakness for the bottle. He would be out for count by now. Shakuni was his daughter. She had run the house ever since her mother died of cancer. She was a good friend. Shakuni had some inkling of the boy's plans. She would not raise an alarm.

The boys clambered into the boat. They shoved off and then used paddles. Balancing the boat could be a tricky affair. The boys had grown up by the river. They would not capsize. Another flash of lightning lit up the lake and gave them their bearings. The rain came down in torrents. Ravi paddled the boat while the boy bailed her out. Water sloshing around inside the boat would slow them down. It would also make the boat more difficult to handle.

It was dark. Lights in the nearby town of Kottayam had been doused for the thunderstorm. Water over the fields was placid. A few fish flitted past their boat, their scales shimmering the silver of a hundred moonlit nights. A crocodile floated past. He opened one hooded eye as the boat swished past. He was not hungry and there was plenty of fish to snack upon. Besides, he knew where the boys were heading.

They could hear the rush of the river ahead. Water was gushing into the fields through gaps in the embankment. The embankment itself was largely under water. They headed further up where water was lapping over a grassy coconut grove. They lugged the small boat across and paused. Thoppil island was downstream. There was a ceaseless sizzle and spray where the island neatly cleaved the rivers rushing waters. They knew what they had to do. Once in the river, they would have to paddle like hell if they were to land on the island.

In the river the current was vicious. Broken tree branches, hollow coconuts and a dead cow swept by. A bee hive bobbed past in the flood water. God help any fisherman who picked it up without realising what it was. Curiosity could sometimes kill. They jumped into the boat and headed for the island. A capsize would be fatal. By the time they righted the boat they would be in the Vembanad lake. The crocodiles would be hungrier there and it would be feeding time. As they reached the island, Ravi jumped ashore. He had the tow rope wrapped around his middle. He held on a tree at the shore line as the boat swung in on his pivot. The boy joined him to lug the boat ashore. They looped the rope around a tree. Flood waters were rising. They would need the boat to paddle back.

The boy felt a thrill of excitement. Ravi was shivering and at end of his tether. They were on Thoppil island. By convention and by law the island was out of bounds. No one ventured there even during the day. There were crocodiles there and snakes in the dense brush. Then there was the Legend. A vicious robber who had escaped the police had tried to take refuge there. His half-eaten body was later scooped out of the lake. The geological society claimed that the islands moorings had been steadily eroding. One of these days, it would crumple and collapse on itself and disappear forever.

The Legend:

There was a time when the rivers of Kerala were highways. Traders and travellers used the river to reach settlements at Kottayam, Alleppy and Kochi. The water was cleaner then, roads did not exist and boatmen were adept. A steady boat and a good boatman were preferred over bouncy bullock carts. Rogue elephants and robbers made the road hazardous. Townships tended to spring up around a rivers banks.

The river was relatively safe in daytime. There were hamlets at points along the river. Travellers could find shelter here at night. These hamlets were well guarded. They charged voyagers for the protection. The river was not safe at night. River pirates, lurked in the bushes along the shoreline with their fast villuvalloms. These men were hardened merciless criminals. Their boats were fast and they killed for loot and for women. River boats were their prime target. On occasion they would raid riverside houses. There were houses by the river line where rich property owners stayed. These households had their defences. River Bandits would raid them only with meticulous planning and armed with insider information. Houses by the river were often of solid wood and stone. You could not break into them. The bandits would burn and smoke the owners out. The modus operandi of setting houses on fire earned them the epithet of fire torch robbers. Once they had the owners in captivity, the robbers would torture the patriarch. This would go on till he told them where the valuables were kept. They would then kill the men before making off with women and gold. Those were violent bloody times.

Legend has it, that a princess from Alleppy once travelled by boat to visit her aunt. It was late. The boatman had suggested that they seek shelter in a hamlet. The girl had insisted that they move on. They had another boat with an armed company accompanying them. These men would protect them from bandits. It was raining heavily by then and the river was soon in spate. A rip current swept both their boats downriver. The old boatman guiding the princess's boat had to use all his skills to keep the boat from going under. The other boat was not so lucky. It capsized, spilling men and goods into crocodile infested waters. Dusk was settling in. A pack of river pirates had followed the boats in stealth. They closed in now. The bandits butchered the men as they tried to right the boat. They then looted what they could from the sinking boat. They could see the old boatman and his dainty passenger downstream.

The old man saw the river pirates. There was little he could do to save the princess. Downriver a large shape loomed out of the water. This was Thoppil island. He manoeuvred the boat to pass around the island. There were rocks here and the hurtling boat squealed as a sharp boulder rent its hull. The boat was now taking in water. There was little time to loose. "Jump", he urged the princess. This island belongs to Thoppil Thankachan. He will keep you safe. The princess jumped down on the rocks. She slipped and fell but managed to catch a low-slung branch. She pulled herself ashore. The boatman smiled. He knew his time was up.

He had done his job. The pirates had not seen the princess jump.

The boat shot past the island wrenched in a eddy current. The pirates gave chase. It was a furlong downriver before they caught up with the boat. They beat the old boatman to pulp and heaved him overboard. They beached the boat on the muddy bank and ransacked it. They had seen the girl on board. Where was she now. "She must have jumped off on Thoppil island", said the leader. "Let's go get her".

Some of the Pirates were hesitant. They had heard of Thoppil Thankachan. The leader laughed at them. "We are ten hardened armed men. No river baron will stand before us". He had seen the girl in the boat. She was worth fighting over. The pirates loaded up their boat with loot and lugged it upriver. A dog followed them. It was the princess's dog Shambu. He had jumped to follow his mistress. He was a little late and had fallen back into the river. There were crocodiles around but they had ignored him. He had managed to reach the river bank. He followed the bandits now and watched as they hid the loot in a small cave by the hill side. The bandits sheathed their swords, jumped into their boat and paddled for Thoppil island.

The princess was sitting on a rock and crying. She had seen the pirates kill the old boatman. She saw them lugging their loot laden boat. Then she saw him. A small dog was following the bandits. He kept his distance from the men. He ducked behind mud piles when they hurled rocks at him. The princess smiled through her tears. Shambu, her dog, was alive.

She turned and ran into the thicket as the pirates launched their boat to the island. They were coming for her. She swore they would never take her alive. She planned to hurl herself to the crocodiles in the river. A man stepped out of the darkness and into her path. He was bronzed and muscular and of medium height. The princess stopped. She knew that this was Thoppil Thankachan. "Don't kill yourself," said the man. "I will save you from the pirates. The princess was brave. She remembered the lore about Thankachan's strength and courage. But he was unarmed and the pirates' carried swords.

There was a shout from the pirates as they landed. They had seen Thankachan and the girl. Thankachan held her by the arm and pulled her behind him. "Go away you dogs", he taunted the charging pirates. I am Thankachan. The pirates stopped. "We will spare you, young man," said the leader. Just hand the girl over. Thankachan was unarmed. He smiled as he confronted the blood thirsty bunch. "She is my princess", he said. "She is going to be my wife", he said. "Now, get off my island".

Shouting an obscenity, the leader of the pirates charged. His sword was held high. His men followed him. Thankachan stepped forward to meet them. He ducked the leader's swinging sword and crushed the man's chest with a crushing blow. As the man fell, dead, Thankachan had his sword. Two pirates who were ahead of the rest seemed to charge past Thakachan. They were headless as the crumpled to the ground. Thankachan smiled as the other pirates turned and ran for the boat.

As the boat shot into the river, Thankachen whistled. There was a flurry of activity as a cluster of crocodiles chased the boat. The pirates saw them coming. The men screamed. They lunged at the armoured heads of the beasts with their swords. The battle was soon over. Their empty boat drifted downriver. Thankachan turned to the sobbing princess. He took her by the hand. He lead her down a path to a clearing. Here, the grass was soft. In the centre of the clearing stood a quaint hut of mud and bamboo. It had a thatched roof. Thankachachan opened the door. She walked into her new home.

The rain stopped. Stars peeked out as the wind pushed dark clouds away. A crescent moon peeked out gingerly. The princess opened the door softly. Thankachan was asleep. She headed for the river. Across the river, Shambu was whining. She would plunge in and swim across to him and bring him to the island. A hand fell on her shoulder. "You are brave, but foolish," said Thankachan. He gave a low whistle. Two large crocodiles slid into the water. Thankachan jumped on one. He sat astride the giant creature as it swam for the shore. The other crocodile followed.

Thankachan followed Shambu to the cave where the pirates stashed their loot. They returned with the princess's possessions. Shambu sat in front of Thankachan on one crocodile. The other one followed with the bags on her back. They were soon back on the island.

The Boy and the legend:

 The past meets the present. Ravi and the boy crept through the brush in the rain. A clutch of squirrels followed them, prancing from branch to branch and chattering with excitement. A wise old owl looked at the boys and hooted once. A large green snake slithered past. The boy looked behind him. Ravi was nowhere to be seen. He had lost his nerve and run back to the boat.

The boy felt no fear. Somewhere ahead, he could hear human voices. Something in the voice seemed strangely familiar. He reached the clearing. There was a hut ahead surrounded by a grassy lawn. A beautiful woman emerged with a steaming bowl in her hands. She called out to the boy. "Come, the Payasam is ready".

A white dog ran across the lawn, wagging his tail as hard as he could. The boy sat on a wooden stool as the dog licked his feet. The lady served him payasam. She then ran her fingers through his hair with affection. "You are growing up fast", she said. "Soon you will be as tall and strong as your great- grand father". A bronzed man ambled out of the door. He lifted the boy in his arms and tossed him in the air before catching him and holding him tight to his chest. He kissed the boy on both his cheeks.

They sat round the table and ate. The payasam was delicious. They walked back to the boat. Ravi was sitting in it. He did not look up as the boy climbed in. Thankachan gave their boat a powerful shove. They crossed the breach in the embankment with ease. Water in the fields was languid. The boy looked around. Ravi was busy paddling. All around the boat fish bobbed out of the water to look at him. A large fish with a torn lip did a little dance, balanced on his tail. "I recognised you when you saved my life. Thank you Thankachen". The fish gave an elaborate bow before diving into the water again. The boat was soon back near the shore. They found the tree where it would be tied. He glimpsed a skirt moving behind the trees. He smiled and waved. Shaguni had waited for them.

The bedroom door creaked a bit as the boy got in. Ricky, his dog came to investigate. Ricky was sniffing at the boy's feet where the white dog had licked him. He looked at his young master with surprise before curling up at his feet. Outside, the rain had stopped. Sunrise was still an hour away.

It was late in the day when the boy woke up. Bfast was puttu and plantains. His father walked in with the newspaper. "Yesterday's floods created havoc. Thoppil island was washed away. After the thunder and lightning and the flash flood, the island has disappeared. I guess that is the end of the myth and the legend". Rikki looked up at his young master and winked. The boy smiled. He was the legend now.

A LOVER'S REQUIEM

Thought that aging brought contentment
Of a life well lived and obstacles overcome
A rationalization of dreams and reality
Brewed in the crucible of earthly experience

Greater skills and higher positions, some look up to me
Targets set and achieved, a demi-fulfillment of goals
Yet there are gaping abysses in contentment, the mind remains unsettled
A belief in one's relevance, actualisation is lacking

Skills are imperfect, the science behind them even more so
We remain dogmatic that our ignorance is wisdom

Basic questions taunt me, the essence,
the meaning of life
It is indeed a play by an idiot, raucous
laughter, meaningless discourse,
endless strife

The petulance of youth has been
replaced by adult scorn
The sweat ripeness of age is rankled by
a pinch of rot
Our bodies go frail and sore, the
energies fade, faculties fail
As we eke out the dregs of mediocre
existence with statins and memantine

Constantly groping for acceptance and
appreciation
Like a lonely dog, eager for a pat
Gone is the bravado of youth- the fears
have multiplied
The fragility of the glass house of
existence is frightening

I await that gleam of brilliance, a
realisation or achievement
That would place me safe beyond the
clutches of malignant mediocrity

I grope, but the eyes are weak and the
mind often numbed
Shuddering I look over my shoulder for
the bolt to the brain or a clutch at the
heart

I wait for the door to open, a glow of
light
As you walk in, to make my life whole
again
At last, the glow I see, I rise to embrace
the vision
In the ecstasy of the embrace, I feel the
last throb of a life that has ebbed past

****

A MORNING STROLL

I was strolling down the road one day
A bright and shiny morn
It had been a great leasurely holiday
My step was light yet strong

Birds chirped in the air
There was a heavenly breeze
I felt no fears, no doubts or care
Just happiness and inner peace

I saw a crowd of toiling men
Heaving upon a rope
A bright blue car had tumbled down
The rocky mountain slope

I stopped and watched the tale unfold
As the men heaved and hawed
Would the rope and the car's axle hold
Was the slumped man inside, dead and
cold

A motley crowd had gathered round

The car was inching up
At last, it reached the level ground
Without a major hiccup

A doctor from the ambulance
Now got the car door wrenched free
A lifeless man inside, he tumbled out
Oh heaven! It was me

Ah well, I could remember now
Driving fast down hill
The rest was a blur, there was a glow
My spirit freed, the battered body lay
still

I could see them now, as they bustled
around
Covered my body with a sheet
They saw me naught, nor heard my
sound
As I whimpered on that lonely hill

My peace was gone, my kin would cry
There would be a crisis and agony
Could I find a way out of this mess
Turn the clock back, not pray the price

I felt a tap upon my shoulder
God's touch was soft and kind
My peace and claim were soon restored
His countenance made me bolder

Could I go back, once more, I asked
I have to pay many debts
Your debts are paid, your time is up, he
said
You can't return, you are dead

****

AMBITION

The race of life, an unequal field
Intense competition, false camaraderie, focused zeal
Focused at self-advancement, not at tangible goals
Moving ahead, hoping the other will trip or slip on a banana peel

Life is short, the race long and winners are few
Those who care and those who dare don't always win
Self actualisation is rarely the goal, it is a nascisstic sin

Are we striving toward a purpose as our ambitions unfold
To positions and power that game playing earn
Leaving behind a hollowness, as we grow old
Lacking tangible achievement, real contributions

Looking back, it's been a race of futility, the victories feel cold
Relationships, love and warmth, are they really true
Intense feelings, warm companionship and a sharing heart
Are they true or are they like the emperors' clothes, an illusion.

******

TEARS OF JOY, SOBS OF PRIDE

There is a swell in the bosom, hairs stand on end
Time stands still, flags flutter in a waft of nationalism
Emotions unfurled, patriotism, pride, a sense of belonging
Nationality, disparity betrothed by geographic accident

Love, affection, possession, subjugation- a spectrum of relationships
The pain of belonging, a parody of faith, bondage of social structuring
The systems work, for lack of logical options
Affections cannot be universal, even canines roam in packs.

We guard domain and boundaries marked by the stench of bullion
Carve pieces of territory, our domain, never truly owned

The walls get higher, till rationality pulls
them down
The hatred bred by isolation, in cauldrons of
identity

Nurture in the bosom of mothering, a family
lineage
We weave a cocoon of protection, for whom
we care
Equal opportunity, they say, no one will deny
us
As we strive for our betterment, in a world
that is unfair

The spectrum of dependence at the extremes
of ages,
Blankets of support in disease injury and pain
Is the bonding we see eternal, or will the race
evolve
Each man for everyone, a common purpose,
shared dreams.

The barbed fences we built, for protection
from wolves
Would loose relevance in a world where rage
is extinct

The basis of bonding that pervades all species
Group, colonies and families, is mothering
just a survival instinct?

Do we need to belong, are our spirits
entwined
In destinies precast, puppets on a string
Is our bonding innate or a construct in a world
hostile
Are there borders in heaven too, drawn up by
Gabriel

****

www.ingramcontent.com/pod-product-compliance
Lightning Source LLC
Chambersburg PA
CBHW020346180726
47991CB00021B/2554